Scaredy Bat

Written by Jonathan Meres

Illustrated by Anders Frang

This book belongs to:

_____

To Lily Ina. The latest little bat — JM

To Viv and Kathryn, with much appreciation — AF

Huge thanks to Jonathan and Anders for fizzing and whizzing with us on this adventure — LDB

Published by Little Door Books 2021
This edition published 2022

ISBN: 978-1-9162054-0-6

Text copyright © Jonathan Meres 2021
Illustrations copyright © Anders Frang 2021

Design and layout by Anders Frang

Printed in China by 1010.

A CIP catalogue record for this book is available from the British Library.

LITTLE DOOR BOOKS
mail@littledoorbooks.co.uk
www.littledoorbooks.co.uk
twitter: @littledoorbooks

Night was fading in the Dark, Dark Wood.

Light was dribbling in and filling up the cracks.
Things were stirring. Wings were whirring.
The sun was yawning. Day was dawning.
It was morning in the Dark, Dark Wood.

But not all creatures were waking and shaking.

In a hollow of the old oak tree, Big Bat, Middle Bat
and Little Bat snuggled up and closed their eyes.

All night long they'd fizzed and whizzed.

Now it was time to rest and dream upside down dreams.

"Can't sleep!" said Little Bat.

"Ssshhh, Little Bat!" said Middle Bat. "It's getting early."

"Yes," said Big Bat. "If you don't go to sleep, you'll be tired in the evening."

Little Bat closed
his eyes much tighter.

But the Dark, Dark Wood
was getting lighter.
Shining brighter.

The air full of buzzing
and humming
and drumming.

Little Bat didn't like it.
Not one little bit.

"Can't sleep," said Little Bat.

"You're not scared of the light, are you?" grinned Big Bat.

"No!" said Little Bat.

"You are! You are!" laughed Middle Bat.

"Scaredy Bat! Scaredy Bat! Ner, ner, ner, ner, ner!"
sang Middle Bat and Big Bat, together.

Little Bat fluttered to the entrance of the hollow.
Knew what he had to do.
Had to show the other two.

Did not find the teasing pleasing.
Knew that it was time for leaving.

"Where are you going?" said Big Bat.

"Outside," said Little Bat, bravely.

"Ooooooooooh!" said Middle Bat.
"Look out for THE BOGEY BAT!"

"And things that go bump in the day!"
said Big Bat.

"Scaredy Bat! Scaredy Bat! Ner, ner, ner, ner, ner!"
sang Middle Bat and Big Bat, together.

Little Bat peered out from the old oak tree.

The Dark, Dark Wood wasn't dark anymore.
Little Bat not feeling quite so sure.

But with a one... two... three...
and an upside down "Wheeeee!"

Wheeee!

he spread his wings...

...and let go.

Little Bat fizzed and whizzed.
Zoomed and varoomed.
Swooped and whooped
and loop-the-looped.

Weaved in and out of branches.
Turned cartwheels in the air.

Little Bat felt brave.
Little Bat felt good.

Little Bat felt like King
of the Dark, Dark Wood.

But just when he thought there was nothing to worry about.

Nothing to hurry, or scurry back home about.

Little Bat had a feeling, he wasn't alone.
Saw something flicker. Heart beating quicker.

Hard not to think that...it must be...

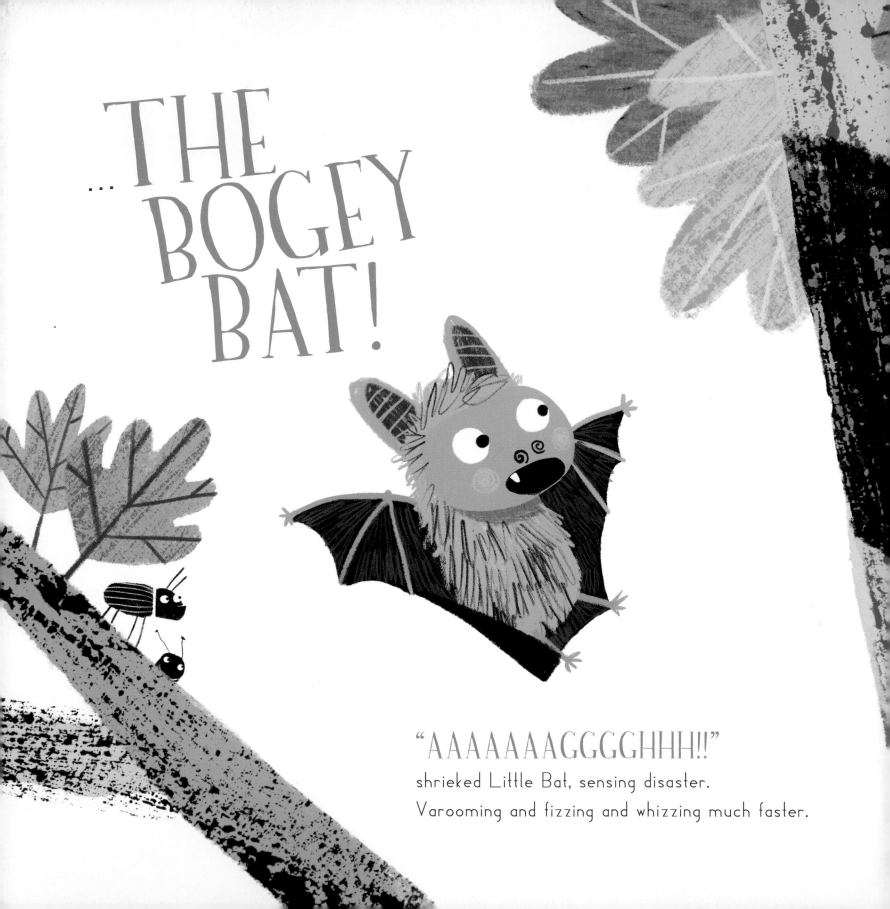

...THE BOGEY BAT!

"AAAAAAAAGGGGGHHH!!"
shrieked Little Bat, sensing disaster.
Varooming and fizzing and whizzing much faster.

But wherever Little Bat flew...
the Bogey Bat flew, too.

Until Little Bat began to see.
There was nothing to be scared of.
The Bogey Bat was just...

...his shadow!

"WHEEEEEE!" went Little Bat, heading for home,
pretending that he'd always known.

Back in the hollow
of the old oak tree,
Big Bat and Middle Bat
started to wonder.

Grew more worried
by the minute.
Wanted Little Bat
back in it.

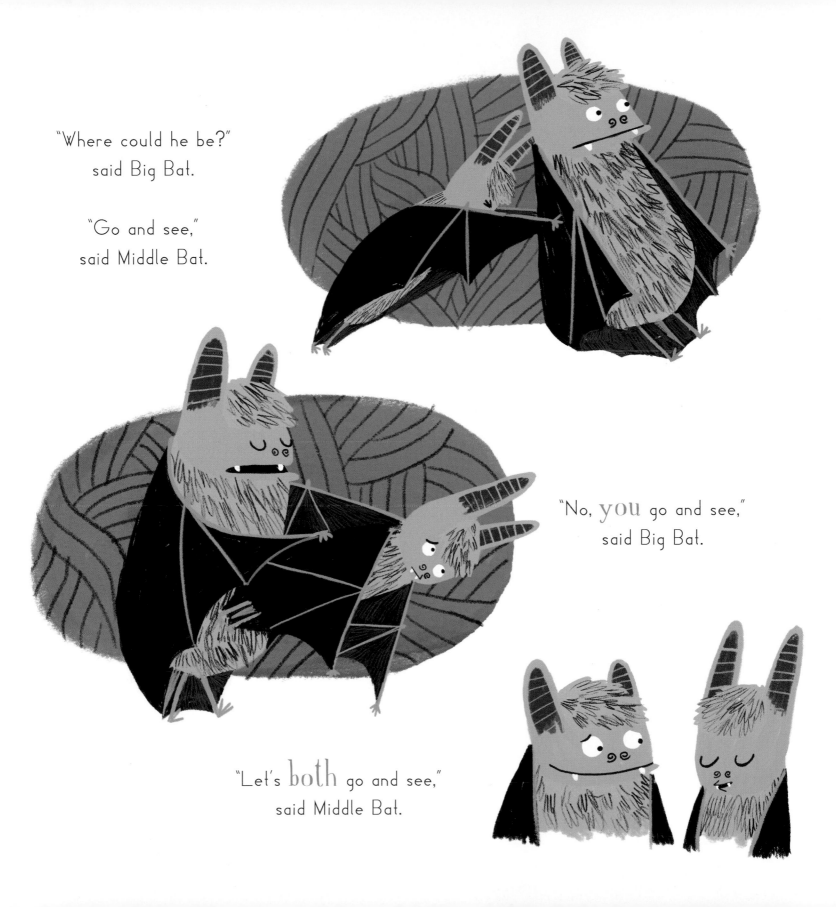

"Where could he be?"
said Big Bat.

"Go and see,"
said Middle Bat.

"No, you go and see,"
said Big Bat.

"Let's both go and see,"
said Middle Bat.

Big Bat and Middle Bat peered out of the hollow.
Both afraid that the other wouldn't follow.

Listening for things that went bump in the day.
They were scared of the light — but they didn't like to say.

Big Bat and Middle Bat watched and waited.
Wishing Little Bat would come back to the tree, again.

And then...

"BOO!!"

went Little Bat, suddenly appearing.

"AAAAAAAGGGGHHHH!!!"
screamed Big Bat and Middle Bat, together.

"Scaredy Bats! Scaredy Bats!"
sang Little Bat, with glee...

...back in the hollow of the old oak tree.